D0607907

DYLAN'S AMAZING DINOSAURS
THE STEGOSAURUS

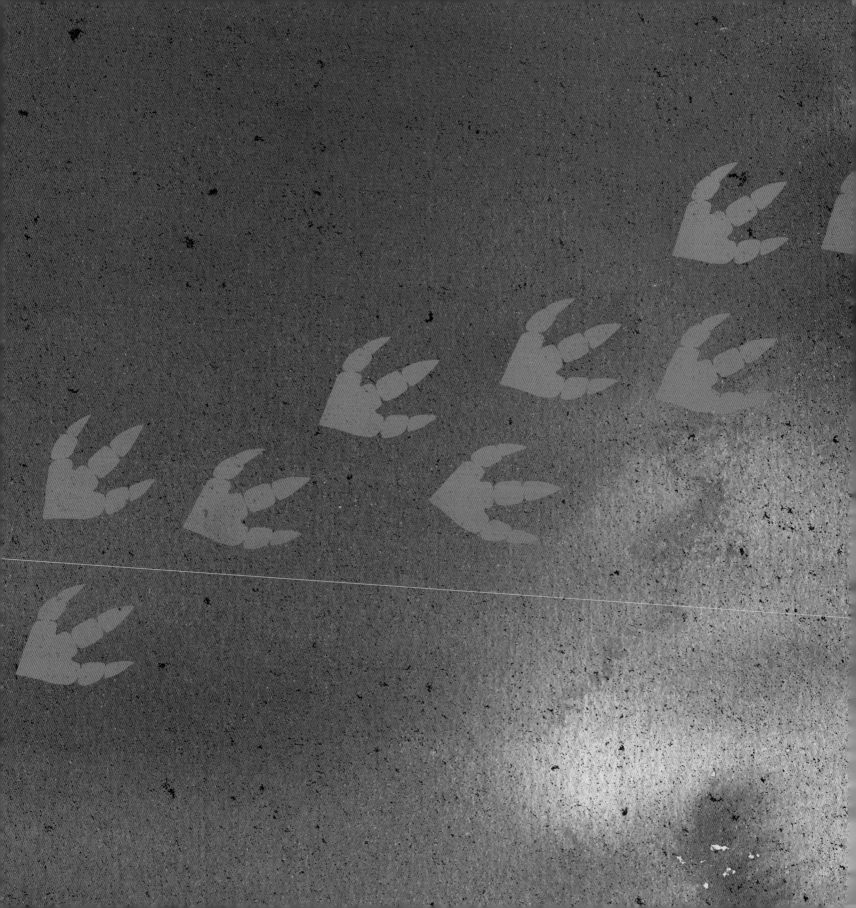

To Tamara, for your wonderful friendship
and extraordinary imagination x—E.H.

For Sam—D.T.

First edition for the United States, its territories and dependencies,
and Canada published in 2015 by Barron's Educational Series, Inc.

First published in Great Britain in 2014 by Simon and Schuster U.K. Ltd., London

Text © copyright 2014 by E.T. Harper
Illustrations © copyright 2014 by Dan Taylor
Paper engineering by Maggie Bateson
Paper engineering © copyright 2014 by Simon and Schuster U.K.

The right of E.T. Harper and Dan Taylor to be identified as the author and
illustrator of this work, respectively, has been asserted by them in accordance
with the Copyright, Designs, and Patents Act, 1988.

All rights reserved. No part of this publication may be reproduced or distributed
in any form or by any means without the written permission of the copyright owner.

All inquiries should be addressed to:
Barron's Educational Series, Inc.
250 Wireless Boulevard
Hauppauge, NY 11788
www.barronseduc.com

ISBN: 978-1-4380-0644-4

Library of Congress Control Number: 2014942965

Date of Manufacture: December 2014
Manufactured by: Leo Paper Products, Ltd., Kowloon Bay,
    Hong Kong, China

Product conforms to all applicable ASTM F-963
and all applicable CPSC and CPSIA 2008
standards. No lead or phthalate hazard.

Printed in China
9 8 7 6 5 4 3 2 1

DYLAN'S AMAZING DINOSAURS

THE STEGOSAURUS

E.T. HARPER AND DAN TAYLOR

BARRON'S

Dylan's tree house was incredible. It was full of extraordinary things, and the most extraordinary of all were Grandpa Fossil's magic Dinosaur Journal and ...

Keep Out!

WINGS, his toy pterodactyl!
"I wonder what amazing dinosaur discovery
we'll make today?" Dylan said as he flung
open the journal.

Fact File

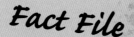

Name: Stegosaurus—or "Roofed Lizard"

Diet: Plants

Habitat: North America and Asia

Unusual features: Triangular plates running from neck to tail. Really small brain . . . the size of a walnut!

Secret Weapon: Thagomizer

Stegosaurus

Thagomizer
?

Plates

"I think we've found our Dino Mission—to find out what a thagomizer is! Let's go Wings!" said Dylan excitedly.

As soon as he heard the magic words, Wings came to life and flew off the shelf.

"Let's go, let's soar . . . off to the land where the dinosaurs roar!" Dylan shouted as they took off from the tree house deck.

"Look there's a group of stegs!

Hmm . . . I wonder what a thagomizer could possibly look like," Dylan thought aloud as they flew over Roar Island. "Could it be like a sword? Or a spike?"

"WOOOOAAAAHHHH!" he cried as Wings swooped over a cliff.

Dylan spotted a lone dinosaur
running as fast as it could along the bank of a river.

"Look at that stegosaurus, Wings!" Dylan exclaimed.

"Wowsers, it's moving fast!"
Dylan soon saw why—just behind it was
an allosaurus in hot pursuit.

But the poor stegosaurus was running out
of steam and slowing down.

"Uh-oh!" Dylan shouted. "It's been separated from the others!
Look, they're on the other side of the river.
If it can just make it to them it will be safe."

"Over there!" he called, jumping and pointing.
"Your herd is just there—

AAARRRGGGHHHH!"

The cliff had crumbled beneath him, and Dylan was sliding straight toward the dinosaurs!

Dylan landed safely on top of the rocks that had fallen down from the cliff.

"Phew, that was close!" said Dylan. "But look, all these rocks have blocked the allosaurus. It can't reach the stegosaurus now!"

But Dylan had spoken a little too soon.
Before the steg could escape, the allosaurus
jumped on top of the rocks and roared.

The stegosaurus stopped to face the allosaurus.
"Oh no, Wings, the only thing that can save the stegosaurus now are those superstrong plates!" said Dylan.

Sure enough the stegosaurus turned to bare its plates toward the approaching allosaurus, and the fight began. THWAAACCCKKKK!

"It may lack brains, but it's definitely brave!" said Dylan as the stegosaurus smashed the allosaurus in the jaw.

THWUUUUUUMMMMPPP!

The allosaurus was strong, though, and knocked down the stegosaurus with one blow. "Come on, Steg!" shouted Dylan. "Get up!"

Just when they thought it was all over, the stegosaurus
used its last bit of energy to whip up its mighty tail and . . .

BANG!

"Wow!" Dylan said. "Look at those spikes;
they're an awesome secret weapon. Hang on! That's it!
They're the THAGOMIZER!"

The allosaurus was knocked out. Wings hopped over the fallen dinosaur as Dylan saw his chance to help the stegosaurus get back to its herd.

"Quick Wings, I have a plan!" he said
as he climbed onto the pterodactyl.

He reached into his backpack and pulled out his lunch.
"Fly close to the stegosaurus, Wings!"

They swooped down, and Dylan bravely put out his hand
to let the huge creature sniff the carrot he was holding.

"That's it, Steg! Come on!"
They flew over a fallen tree, dropping
a trail of carrots along it.
The stegosaurus crunched them one by one
and crossed to the safety of its herd.

"Time to go home, I think," said Dylan.

As the pair flew over the cliff top, the allosaurus' eyes opened—it had spotted them!

"Higher, Wings!" Dylan yelled.

They soared upward just as the dino's jaws snapped beneath them.

"Dino Mission accomplished!" Dylan shouted triumphantly as they launched themselves head first back into the tree house.

"That stegosaurus' secret weapon is pretty cool," he said, sketching the picture of the thagomizer into the Dinosaur Journal.

As he closed the journal, he turned to say good-bye to his faithful flying friend.

"You're my secret weapon, Wings!" Dylan smiled, and crunched the last carrot.

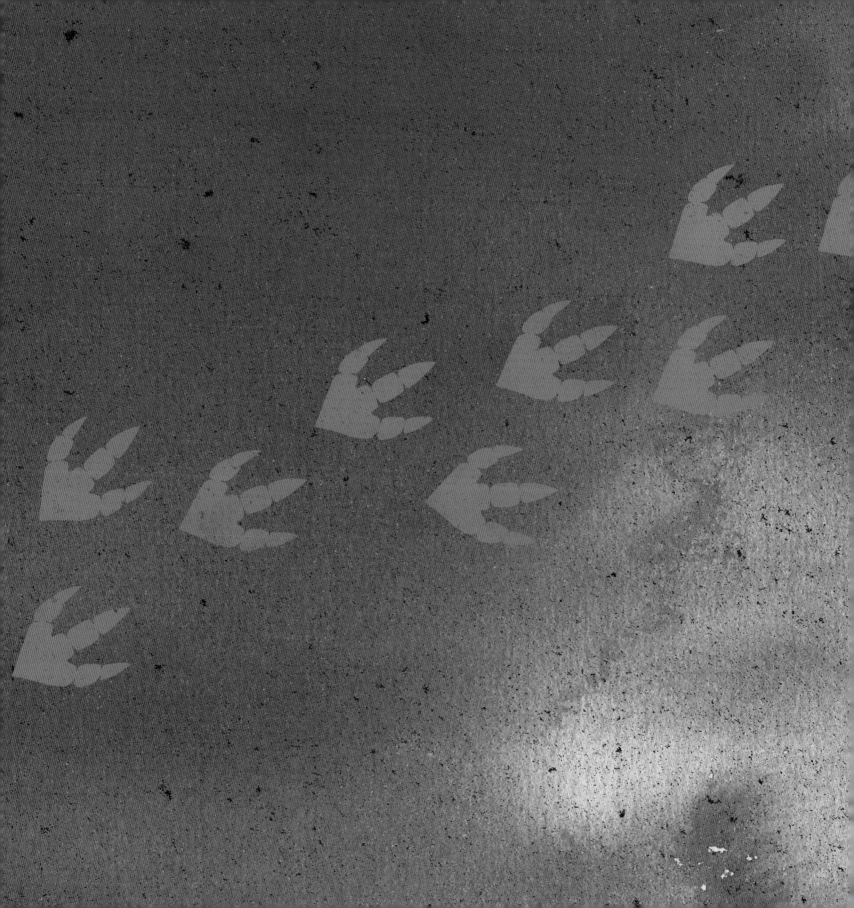

LOOK OUT FOR MORE AMAZING ADVENTURES
WITH DYLAN AND WINGS!

OUT NOW—
THE TYRANNOSAURUS REX